Claudine

Claudine

A Fairy Tale for Exceptional Grownups

by Marian Grudko *and* T.A. Young

Drawings by Donal Partelow

and paintings of Paris by Renée Gauvin

138 In Progress Publishing
New York

Claudine

www.138inprogresspublishing.com
mariangrudko@138inprogresspublishing.com

Claudine illustrations by Donal Partelow
donalpartelow@gmail.com

First Edition: November 2019
Printed in the United States of America

Library of Congress Control Number: 2019905272
ISBN: 978-0-9982768-7-8

The authors wish to thank Elizabeth Wilson for graciously allowing us to use a quote from her book, *Adorned in Dreams*.

Cover and interior paintings by Renée Gauvin
www.artbyreneegauvin.com

Book formatted by Elliot Toman, www.asubtleweb.com

For Michèle "Michou" Morin, teacher and friend
- M.G.

To Mrs. Malubier, Victrola, and Maximus
- T. A. Y.

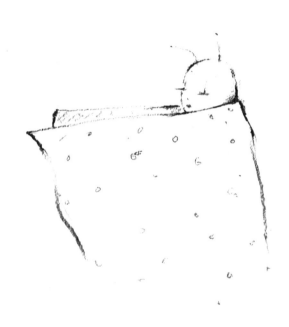

· One ·

Divine Tailor
Clothe me
Change me
Lose me
Find me
Your raiment is
My being.

Claudine was a ladybug who wanted more than anything to live in Paris. Surely, she belonged there. Her red and black ensemble was equal to any creation from the House of Dior. And surely she would be noticed by the greatest directors of film: she bore a striking resemblance (did she not?) to the beautiful actress, Marion Cotillard.

When Claudine flew amongst the flowers in her garden, she didn't see that modest place in the French countryside. No, the garden was Paris in spring; the little path was the rue de Rivoli; and the fireflies beside the small stream were the lights along the Seine.

Each day, Claudine went to a rosebush, otherwise known as the Café de Flore. She thought of the moment when some grand literary personage would come, take one look at her, and begin his masterpiece, inspired by the mysterious air of that ravishing *coccinelle*.

Sometimes Claudine spoke aloud to the characters of her imagination.

"Oh my darling, I wait for you..."

The other ladybugs who shared the rosebush thought her somewhat frayed around the borders.

"A head full of clouds, that Claudine," they said.

Claudine heard them. "No," she thought. "A head full of Paris!"

That night, Claudine packed a suitcase with her most precious possessions: a portrait of herself, a mirror, and the complete works of Simone de Beauvoir.

The next morning, Claudine flew to the station to take the train to Paris.

On the train was a tiny woman. She wore a black dress with a scarlet scarf. Claudine admired her immensely.

"Hello!" said Claudine. "I am going to Paris!"

"Of course!" said the little woman. "But first, you will need shoes."

Claudine closed her eyes. She pictured herself on a grand boulevard, wearing the shoes of her dreams: white, with red polka dots, and very high heels...

"You must go to a shop," continued the woman, "very near the rue du Faubourg Sainte-Antoine. It is in a narrow alley that is easy to miss. But look carefully, and once you have found it, ask for Pierre." Then she smiled enigmatically.

Claudine opened her eyes. "Who is Pierre?" she asked.

But at that moment, the train arrived at the North Station, and the little woman had disappeared.

"What happened?" asked Claudine. Then she shuddered. "The woman was a ghost!.. or... oh, la la - she was kidnapped by a frightful man with a hook...or maybe she left like that simply because she was rude..."

In any case, the little lady departed quite precipitously: she had dropped her scarf, and left it behind. Claudine could not lift the whole thing, but she thought she should take a piece of it as a clue for the police, should that prove necessary. She imagined herself dressed in a tiny trench-coat, with a Fedora worn low, half-covering her eyes...

The doors of the train opened. Quickly, Claudine took a pair of scissors from the sewing kit in her valise. She cut a small piece of silk fabric from the inside of the scarf.

"It does seem," thought Claudine, "that this piece of silk would make a perfect scarf for me." And she draped it artfully around her neck.

Now she felt truly ready for Paris - except for shoes.

When she dis-embarked, the bustle of the station was overwhelming; she had never seen so many of anything be-fore. People were moving about with urgency and intensity,  hugging and lugging their children, dogs, and valises as they half-ran in every direction. Claudine loved it, the color, the en-ergy, the excitement: it was contagious. Even though her suit-case was growing so heavy that flight was soon to be impossible, she didn't care: she would use her legs like everyone else in

Chapter I

Paris. And if you must walk, you need the right footwear. She would find Pierre to begin her transformation into a genuine Parisian. (How could she know that this transformation had already begun and that her wings were already shrinking, as if her mind was determined to make them vestigial? Feet were the way to go and she had four more than everyone else. Deep down inside, she thought that might have to be rectified, too, if for no other reason than the cost of buying shoes by the half-dozen.)

She reckoned: "Pierre is not a common name in France, so finding a Pierre who owns a shoe store should not be too difficult. And, really, how many shoe stores can there be in Paris?"

In her defense, there have been worse miscalculations based on ignorance, but this acknowledgment does nothing to abbreviate the amount of time it took Claudine to find the right Pierre. It was days.

At last she found the street, the rue du Faubourg Sainte-Antoine. The clicking of all those heels reminded her of the cicadas back home. The alley had its own name: rue de Glace; and this tiny street intersected another called L'Avenue de Vanité. One should not read too much into this.

The alley was difficult to find; she walked past it three times before she could see its entrance. Of course the store was *magnifique*! A salesperson approached her, thinking at first that someone had spilled a drop of strawberry sorbet. When he saw that it was a ladybug, he called for Pierre.

Pierre was everything one would expect him to be, sans monocle. He seemed to have invisible plumage. He clicked and clucked as he walked.

"And what may we do for you, Mademoiselle Ladybug?

"Sir, I was told you could provide me with some shoes... that would make me worthy of the streets of this great city...that would make me a woman of Paris."

" 'A woman of Paris.' I see. And may I ask why? I for one see no advantage of one over the other." He raised his hands palms up as if weighing Woman of Paris and Ladybug.

"If either has an advantage over the other, I would say I have it." She fluttered her wings and rose a bit. "But sometimes change requires sacrifice." She settled back to the floor. "If I wish to be part of this great city, this may not be the right... um...look for it. Ladybugs may not be taken seriously among the literati, the artistes, the fashioned."

"Madame, to quote the great Simone de Beauvoir, 'One is not born a woman, but becomes one.' We shall make you a Parisian, providing you with the requisite footwear. Follow me. We have a department for just such, shall we say, challenges as yours. Be confident that you are not the first, er, convert to humankind. I, myself, am quite familiar with the process."

To quote Pierre, "Why dwell on the process? We sell outcomes!" After an hour with this master, Claudine was what she asked to be. She looked in a mirror and was mesmerized...and afraid. She looked back at the approving Pierre: "I'm not sure," she said, "two legs..."

"But two fabulous legs, mademoiselle. And as a woman you are quite lovely. You remind me of a certain actress."

"But two?" It seemed difficult to balance, but given the more precarious support system and the height of the heels a little wobbliness was understandable.

"I remind you of what Madame de Beauvoir said: 'Change your life today, don't gamble on the future, act now - without delay.' This is no time for vacillations: Embrace! Enjoy!"

He crowed with pride at the transformation before him.

It was not long after that Claudine found herself sitting in the Café Littéraire, half-stirring a cocktail and half-smoking a long cigarette in a longer cigarette holder. She had already mastered the look of ennui that was requisite for smoke-filled lounges, cafes, and ateliers. Around her was the usual listless hum of the bored being served by the disenchanted, silently sharing their mutual disdain.

She was waiting for Luzelle, a young woman, - bourgeois, with the mascara of the proletariat – and just charming enough to be forgiven. Luzelle was raised well enough to know that she should arrive just short of being intolerably late.

Also, she was profound. She wrote for a socialist newspaper, had several degrees from prestigious universities that her parents sent her to so she could learn to be profound and they got their money's worth. Men were transfixed, though really for her beauty; women were transfixed, but really in envy. Claudine was transfixed because she was a ladybug and new to town. (But *vraiment*, what is it that defines a ladybug? Is it really a matter of legs and wings and colors? Is that what defines them...or us?)

Luzelle sighed. Sighs were a form of punctuation for her; she had many variations and she ladled her sentences with these susurrations: she was clearly not only profound, but a tortured soul living in a world that could only fall short of her expectations. (Luckily, the world has more important things to do than to prove the likes of Luzelle to be wrong, wrong in that shallow, self-absorbed way that makes the world at least consider dropping her down a volcano.)

Anyway, she sighed. "We live in a vortex, my dear, a vortex."

Claudine asked, "A vortex?"

"Yes - a whirlpool of hypocrisy and naiveté and ignorance. We puff on our cigarettes" (she mindlessly puffed on her cigarette) "and we drink our little drinks" (she mindlessly drank her little drink) "and we watch the people come and go before us as if walking in circles, Dantesque circles. A well-dressed purgatory."

"Oh, that's terrible," said Claudine noticing a stunning dress walking by, red with black polka dots that....she rose suddenly, but Luzelle was too absorbed in the motion of the cigarette smoke to notice. Claudine ran after that dress as best she could, for her two feet were killing her, and before the dress could turn the corner at Place du Coin, she was close enough to say "excuse me" at a pardonable decibel level.

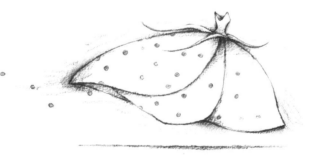

The woman in the dress did not look bothered by the interruption in her stride; in fact, when she turned to face Claudine, she showed only patience. "Claudine," she said, "go back to Pierre. You look miserable. You don't match. You don't match at all." She touched Claudine's cheek, and sped on.

Claudine studied her reflection in the window of Jacques Malubier's Salon des Robes and she felt sorrow for a lost one, which some might think inexplicable given these circumstances.

She recalled sitting on a leaf as it rose and fell like a branch in a lake, gently, rhythmically, as the sun slipped behind the trees and the deer peered out to begin their twilight foraging.

In the end, she found Pierre to be entirely sympathetic. He told her that he was tempted to go with her, but how could Paris survive without him, and that she should not be a stranger. He said that being a ladybug and living in Paris are not incompatible if one is willing to live a humble life. But then again, if you want to live a humble life, why bother coming to Paris?

A humble life. That lovely twilight image, day fading, colors dimming, darkness defeating light...At that moment twilight began to sneak its way into the city. Claudine's senses told her that her city – her city! – was taking a brief rest before the night began. There was a moment of silence as if it were a solemn time, the time that the numberless lights went on in streets and homes and restaurants and cafes. If she were still naïve, she would have thought that stars had come to share in the night's festivities. As if the axis of the universe were the Eiffel Tower; as if that monument were a celestial maypole around which all things danced and spun.

No. What is not compatible are the City of Lights and the humble life! Are lions humble? Are oceans? Are stars? Then why ladybugs? I have not come here to live in the shadows, to hide among the nondescript, the invisible - nor shall I leave!

"Monsieur, I am meant to be a ladybug. Not a lady. Why must I compromise and be only half of myself? I shall be my entire self as I feel myself to be, and live as I feel I ought to live. Fireflies do not settle! Moths do not settle - they are simply too drunk to know the difference between a light bulb and the moon, which explains all those concussions - but they believe they are shooting for the moon and they are racing toward it full throttle! They are committed to their goal. As am I!"

With a hug that demonstrated unusual emotion for a rooster, Pierre bid her to take off her shoes. She did, and immediately her feet floated from the floor. He looked at her as she levitated. "I will come up with a compromise, but there is no compromise in fashion. We make statements, not concessions. Perhaps that is why I understand well what you are saying. So we have some work to do, the two of us, to make you ready for Paris under your own terms. Very well then."

With gratitude and relief, Claudine - restored to her former self - first wiped away a tear, and then took her mentor's hand.

Two

Dress is the frontier between the self and the not-self.
- Elizabeth Wilson, *Adorned in Dreams*

"...and that, Claudine, shall be the last tear we shed," Pierre asserted, though his reluctance to release her hand suggested a less-than-stoic rooster. "Now comes the difficult part, for you have chosen your path, but not your means of conveyance. You will travel by both foot and wing; but will you be hoisted on the shoulders as a hero or with your own petard, which is invariably the fate of those with the conjoined qualities, vanity and shallowness?"

Claudine could not understand the gravity of Pierre's voice. She knew her conveyance: the adulation of the fashion folk. She would ride the runway into the heart of that world. She had no interest in vanity and shallowness: her focus was beauty, fashion, style, mirrors, cameras, cosmetics and silk. Claudine tried to collect her thoughts. Fear and excitement, joy and...more joy! The fear came from the freedom. She was unfettered from society's definition of her. Now she could create herself.

But she needed the perfect vehicle. The answer – of course! - Paris Fashion Week! Claudine would design...would wear...would...do it all! She was so distracted by her ambition, she hit her head on the ceiling.

Pierre would help her, to be sure, but was it fair to ask? He, too, would be part of the Haute Couture shows at the Carrousel de Louvre. How could she ask him to compete against himself? For his part, he knew what she was thinking and found her ethical conflict endearing. He smiled at the thought of ethics clearly having made a wrong turn to end up in the fashion room, where claws and stingers were wet with the blood of best friends. He would have helped her. For the moment, he said nothing, not wanting to taint the experiment.

That night she made a list of those who could help her and there turned out to be quite a few: spiders who could weave the finest threads; worms that were magical spinners; frogs who had transformed themselves into princes; ugly ducklings; in short, all critters metamorphosed, transmuted, reshaped, and restyled, by nature or by magic.

She would have to return to a natural place, a garden, but she knew it was there that she would find what she needed. She saw the irony in this, but irony always makes ladybugs contemplate the true meaning of existence, which only fuels the creative fires.

Claudine - who never did anything by halves - decided to visit the Bois de Bologne, that grand park in Paris which embraces a tad over two thousand acres of much natural goodness, including all the creatures mentioned so far in this story.

One evening she was in the company of Shimmy The

Spider and he asked her what all of this was for. "I want to create for the same reason you do," she replied.

"To catch food?" he asked.

"Well, no. Not at all."

"Then your reason.....?"

"Aren't you proud of your webs?"

"Proud? I never give it a thought. I build my webs to the best of my ability. If I fall short, the consequences are not good: I cease to exist. You do your best because you must. I can't imagine otherwise. I know of no creature who would do less than he or she could. Even for our most futile efforts we apply all that is inside of us."

In the ensuing silence, a leaf fell from the top of a maple tree and floated to the ground.

Shimmy was right. Claudine realized her motives should not be matters of ambition, but of integrity. Nature does not create mountains and forests to brag about them. This realization brought Claudine's momentum to a halt. Here was the sticking point: How could being true to herself and being true to Nature be incompatible? Luckily, this philosophical conundrum was easy to shake off, because she had an ensemble to create.

When her work was complete, there was quite a crowd to witness its unveiling. All who had helped Claudine were present, and many who had heard of this event, attended: rabbits, ants, skunks, foxes, snails, worms, snakes, flies, birds, beavers, deer...It was enough to have Claudine's heart pounding.

Chapter 2

Yet, taste is a tricky thing. How would Claudine's round figure be perceived, fitted into what appeared to be a rainbow cocoon replete with patches of fur; her sleeves a hybrid of dolman and bishop styles; a skirt decorated with godets that splayed a puffy polonaise skirt over her ruching shibori shift that lent a crimped and crinkled effect to the satin and crinoline fabric, reminiscent of spectral figures in flowing, tattered nightgowns; an audacious rickrack bustle; shimmering raffia cords on a grosgrain gingham apron; tassels short and long falling from her corded tiara over a turban of felt; a bateau neckline blended seamlessly with a bolero jacket fastened with gems and coral; hints of indigenous flora, and smudges of...was that spoiled avocado? She also wore a monocle.

The next day, Anastasie the Worm, resident Bois de Bologne critic, wrote in her column: "Heavens! It looked like a wildly flamboyant-yet-grungy homeless snake had swallowed a bowling ball with jittery legs! I immediately knew that I was looking at *The Very Next Big Thing!*" Claudine was off to the races.

Would the reception be the same among the human population?

On her way out of the park, she felt a spasm of loneliness. The question changed for her: it was no longer, "Would Paris love her work as much as those whose homes were not made of brick?" It was, "Would she be as happy receiving the adulation of the bipedal Parisians?" Imagine the difference between asking *who* matters rather than *what* matters?

Would Claudine return ready to win that city or would she decide that who really mattered was back in the park? She recalled the time she stepped down from the train and felt her feet touching her glorious city. The train seemed to steam and stomp like an impatient horse driven to move, finding stillness intolerable, though she could have been reading into things, prone as she was to pathetic fallacy.

She allowed herself one more such fallacy: she believed the train had been confident in itself and in its direction. Maybe it was the tracks, which she presently envied. She had only the enormous spoke wheel of new direction, her new destiny, perhaps - if there is such a thing as a new destiny: isn't it all part of the same destiny, if you believe such things?- or perhaps those spokes were rays of light expanding outward, meaning hope.

Claudine, Claudine: you have ahead of you so many opportunities to make the wrong decision.

She once heard a poem, by an American, something about the road less traveled. Surely it was less traveled, because it was not as good? The thought of roads caused Claudine to look down at her feet. She had not made shoes! For these, the human Parisians had no peer. She remembered a pair she had seen in Pierre's shop: Christian Loboutin Last Empress d'Orsay pumps in laser-cut patent leather over red suede underlays finished with covered buckle straps and six-inch spike heels - who could resist? She would ask Pierre to fit her with multiple pairs. Surely this would complete her outfit, and would be the compromise he had promised?

We'll delve into the advantages and disadvantages of trains and tracks and all manner of paths another time. But just a taste: you know the road less traveled? Oh, my dears, there's a reason for that!

· Three ·

Works without show, and without pomp presides...
- Alexander Pope, *Essay on Criticism*

When the famed fashion shrew (you may take this literally given the context) Diane Frois-d'Hiver heard about this new creature sending her flock of French fashionistas into a collective tizzy, she pelted her underlings with whatever she could find on the editor's desk to drive them to find this upstart crow, Claudine. "Crow, ladybug, *quelle est le difference*? Find her!"

And out they ran as paper clips and 8x10's flew overhead. Before the next sentence could be completed, Claudine was standing in Frois d'Hiver's office.

The editrix studied Claudine. "I don't see it. No, wait, I do see it. No, I thought I did, but...ah, there it is..." Somewhere in Paris, paint dried.

Finally, she came to the point. "You shall be in my show tomorrow. Whatever plans you thought you had, cancel them. You will be our special guest. You may thank me later. Go to this address." Frois-D'Hiver gave Claudine a business card and immediately – or so Claudine felt – Claudine ceased to exist. She waited a few seconds, just in case, then she left.

The frenzy of the dressing room behind the stage was

deceptive in that it was robotic. Even the epithets that peppered the exchanges seemed mechanical. Models, hair stylists, cosmeticians, toucher-uppers, gophers (yep), sewers and stitchers, photographers, choreographers, reporters, and the pythons of the industry, agents, glared at each other coldly like energy-efficient interrogation lights.

Claudine looked at the models: they looked like intolerant baguettes.

She stood next to what appeared to be a stunning host to a tapeworm and ventured to have a conversation, beginning with a harmless observation: "It's terribly cold in here. Is that deliberate?"

No response.

"Is it to keep the makeup from running?" It could have been a joke.

The stunner pouted at Claudine. "Darling, it is cold in here because it is cold in here."

"Well, yes, I suppose. But..."

"Darling, you believe you are one of those warm, sensitive types, with....what is the name of that organ?...ah, yes, a heart. Whatever are you doing here?"

"I'm one of the mod..."

"Darling, I know that. I mean why would you be here if you seek warmth?"

"Don't people here have feelings?

"Feelings, darling, are fattening." She turned back to the mirror.

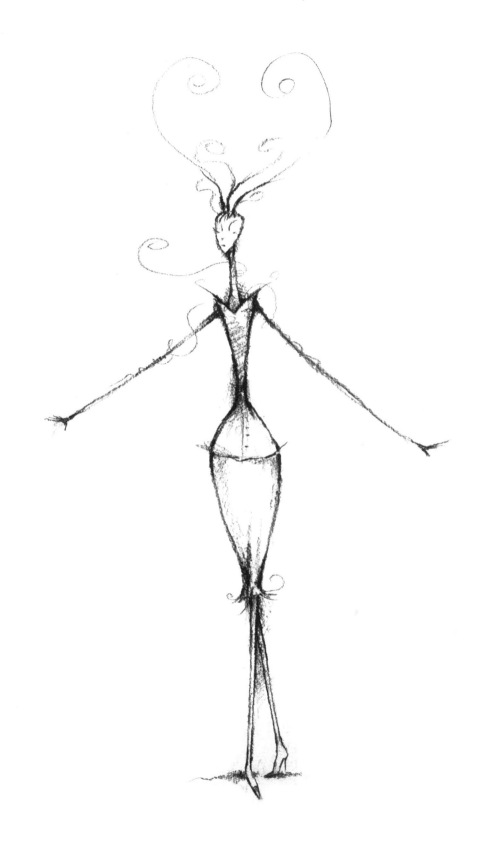

In ten minutes, Claudine received more attention than she had in her life. She tried to find fault with this, but she could not. She watched herself being painted and primped and prepped for the runway and the anticipation that even more attention would be given her made her feel like royalty. The compliments were endless; she was told over and over again that she was stunning, breathtaking, fabulous, striking, dazzling, the living embodiment of Aphrodite, Venus, Marion Cotillard.

She positively owned the runway: who knew legs could move like that? She floated and who knew that would come in so handy? The entire front row lowered their heads to see the space between Claudine and the floor.

Back in the dressing room, glowing with joy, she saw in the mirror the reflection of dear, dear Pierre. She cried out, "Oh, Pierre! Did you see? Did you see how they all love me?"

"Are you happy?"

"Why I've never been happier! Oh, but I have a feeling I've done something wrong, judging from that pout."

"It's nothing." Pierre could easily have executed an extemporaneous diatribe on the matter of what matters, but the greater matter was, did she deserve to have her ship sunk, and to what avail. So he said, "Let us celebrate your triumph. Meet me at that little cafe by my shop and we shall do so."

"Oh, that would be lovely." After saying these words, both she and Pierre had the same thought: this was not the voice of Claudine.

Hours later, Pierre was paying the tab at the little cafe by his shop, when Claudine came running in and began drenching him with apologies. "Oh, Pierre, as soon as you left, Ms. Frois-D'Hiver grabbed me by the arm and simply would not let go. She introduced me to so many glorious people..."

Pierre never looked at her. He walked out of the cafe with Claudine following fast behind him. "Wait...."

Pierre stopped and turned to her. "Claudine, it pains me to say I have lost someone whom I was quite fond of, a delightful little creature who wants so much to be something she is not. Dreams are wonderful things, but – as they say – achieving them is rarely good for long. A dream captured is a dead dream. So, whoever you are, *adieu.*"

Terrible words, thought Claudine. What a small, petty, jealous creature Pierre has turned out to be. Good riddance to him. Then she cried and cried and cried. When she tried to call Frois-D'Hiver, her secretary told her that she was unavailable.

Behind her, the cafe's lights went out and even Claudine's shadow abandoned her. And worse, Claudine was foolish enough to wonder where her happiness had gone when it had so suffused her only moments ago.

· Four ·

Time has passed like a courier with urgent news.
But that's just our simile.
The character's invented, his haste is make-believe,
his news inhuman.

"View with a Grain of Sand" by Wislawa Szymborska
translated by S. Baranczak and Clare Cavanagh
Northwestern University Press, 1991

There is a leaf – you need not imagine it for it is real – a leaf that weakened a bit, faded a bit, yellowed a bit, then fell spinning to the ground, where it went from its sallow yellow-green to brown, and all the moisturizer in the world could not keep it from becoming dried out and brittle.

Barely a season ago, Claudine sat on this leaf.

Now the leaf, after being carried aloft many miles, found itself in Paris, pushed by lesser winds along the 6th arrondissement, the Saint-Germain quartier, a stone's throw from the Jardin du Luxembourg, the very streets where Sartre and de Beauvoir drank coffee and expounded – a kinder word than droned - tirelessly to all who would listen; and where Camus and Hemingway veered and tottered, nursing black eyes and cut lips, and kicking around the odd metaphor. These magnificent beings were the living embodiments of Rimbaud's *Bateau Ivre*, the drunken boat, floating rudderless down indifferent rivers.

But why discourse on one little leaf that had some brief history with Claudine? Because here—in the 6th arrondissement—we find both the leaf and Claudine within a hair's width of each other, for Claudine had taken a little apartment, originally a simple affair, but now boasting a modern kitchen, charming floral fabrics, prints in red and ivory, light furniture: a warm, quaint business with a tiny wrought-iron balcony that once offered a clear view of besotted, tottering expatriates.

—

If Nature worked the way it was supposed to, Paris this night would have been subjected to a drenching, wind-swept rain, perfectly reflecting Claudine's state of mind. But this being real life – and real life is never as neatly written – it was merely drizzling. The paltry precipitation gave the boulevards of Paris a sheen that turned the usually gentle illumination of the streetlights into glaring, discomforting affairs that made one wince and turn away.

People do not learn lessons quickly; it takes a long time, not for reflection, but for acknowledgment. One does not say, "Ah, now I know." Rather one says, "I wish I knew then," adding wistfully, "but it would have been impossible to know then what I know now." Retrospect is a distant lens.

Pierre knew this. All the wisdom in the world could not have saved Claudine. Were you to visit her now, in her little cottage in Cherbourg, she would speak to you as she moved about her garden, alighting on this flower or that, and smile at her silliness, her naiveté. And mention Pierre: her smile would broaden in perfect contradistinction to her sorrow. One could easily believe she saw or sought to see her old friend in those flowers.

We were discussing the problematic suitability of a misty Paris night to a lost ladybug. That night, she took breaks from feeling sorry for herself to feel anger towards Pierre, who had dashed her night of success and attendant elation into little shards of reflective glass. Be assured there was no reflection going on within Claudine; if she were a hornet, Pierre would have been skewered: he was a heartless, selfish, jealous cad.

As an aside, the rain could not have cared less.

Pierre was seated in his apartment on rue de Jean-Paul-George, wearing his smoking jacket, swirling his cognac, and regretting his big mouth. Was that the right time for that lesson? Sheer arrogance. Sheer ignorance. He had no difficulty finding faults in his behavior. Of course, tomorrow he would apologize. The fool. No: two fools, he thought. Funny how wisdom can be a terrible quality; for example, he knew that the morning would make the world intolerable to both damaged parties.

Now he stood before the fireplace and studied the photographs on the mantle. And now he absently scanned his bookshelves. And now he recalled a line of poetry by John

Crowe, who added the surname Ransom when he joined the human race. It went like this: "There was such speed in her little body, And such lightness in her footfall, It is no wonder her brown study Astonishes us all." He wondered why that particular line came to mind, then realized it was the phrase "brown study," for this was precisely his state of mind: melancholy and contemplative.

He would make amends: if it was fame she wanted, he would get it for her; he had a good friend in the famed director, Charles Chopin, a clever British chap who suffered from Francophilia. He—Pierre—would ask Chopin to give her a frame or two, as a flower girl, perhaps, or clerk or star-struck ingenue or waif. Chopin would know.

But Pierre must see Claudine tonight. He must, for the silly little fool needed him. This was not his usual arrogance speaking, this was an arrogance of another sort, infused as it was with the genuine concern that is camouflaged as

28

condescension. "A soul as lost as hers...." No, not lost: misplaced by *her*. He scanned the shelves of his library and realized that this was not a rare blunder.

A few drops of rain and brandy later, and Pierre was off to save the signatory damsel in distress as designated by the knight-in-shining-armor code (article 2, section 3, paragraph 4.)

On his way, Pierre ran into the last person he wanted to run into: Rita Braywiss, veteran dilettante and gossip; yes, such individuals are the indispensable lubricant that keeps high society high.

"Pierre!" she shrieked, cracking several windows nearby and driving four unsuspecting dogs to suicide. "Have you heard?" (These are the words that seem to preface a story about other people, but in fact are the parlance of the solipsist, whose philosophy denies the existence of other people.)

"That little so-and-so who everyone is making a fuss over ... Claudelle ... Claudette ... Clauless ..."

"Claudine."

"Yes, the very same!

Pierre felt dread and showed none of it. He said, "Go on."

"It turns out that she's ... she's ..." (her voice became a whisper) "...she's a ladybug!

Pierre felt relief and showed none of it. "You don't say."

"I don't know the entire story, yet, but it will come out. It's too horrible. She'll be gone and forgotten in a flash."

Pierre felt loathing towards Rita but, well, you know.

"Rita, *chèrie*, I must be going. We shall meet for a drink

soon, yes? So sorry. Until soon."

We pause for a flash of Shakespearean lightning. (Pause.) And we're off again.

Pierre knocked on the door. Claudine knew who it was, probably because of the lightning. She invited him in and they sat opposite each other in simple chairs set close to the radiator; the warmth was nice.

"I ran into our friend Rita just now."

"Then you've heard the latest. Pierre, do you find irony in this?"

"I enjoy my irony with more sense. No matter. The phone shall ring again." He raised his finger in absurd triumph.

"Pierre, I've grown tired of this society."

"Well, it has been nearly a month. Your patience is admirable."

"I need something with more...more substance. More meaning. I shall become an actress."

Were we not just discussing irony moments ago?

"Well." That's all Pierre could muster as a response.

Claudine took his hand. "I will be discovered! Do you not think so?" She glanced in the mirror.

Pierre was beguiled, not for the first time, by their apparent synchronicity of thought. "Of course you will. You shall be an actress!" He raised the finger of absurdity again. "I know a rather famous fellow, in fact. I shall arrange a meeting." Claudine glowed, which is atypical behavior for a ladybug, and Pierre was happy to see it.

Pierre looked at her. Was she wearing the perfume he had given her, Florissima Chérie? "May I recite for you a few lines of poetry by a brilliant Polish writer? I find them wonderfully apropos."

"Please do." She sat and made herself look interested, though the important part of the conversation was now over.

"And all this beneath a sky by nature skyless

in which the sun sets without setting at all

and hides without hiding behind an unminding cloud.

The wind ruffles it, its only reason being

That it blows.'"

He waited. She eventually realized that she should respond: "How lovely."

Pierre was going to ask her if... but then he realized how silly that would be: "its only reason being that it blows." He said to himself, "Claudine is a ladybug. What else could she be?" This was Pierre being the sensible creature he was; then out came Nature with a capital N: suddenly comb and beak and wattles and feathers appeared, and Pierre was hopping and flapping and his tail feathers and wings were spread for battle. He roared as only a rooster can roar. He wanted to tell her to grow up, to see what matters, to see anything that was not Claudine! He kicked and scratched, put a couple of gashes into the rug, and his senses returned: The futility of such words to one such as she!

Of course, it is possible that Pierre was jealous: how could he compete for Claudine's attention when Claudine was so enamored with....Claudine?

Claudine had only the barest idea of what had just happened. She gazed at Pierre, then at her shredded carpet, then at the odd feather or two still floating in the air.

"Pierre!"

"I'll pay for your rug." This was said sulkily; futility takes a toll on one's fuel stores.

Pierre smiled, gathered himself, bowed and left, promising again to help her. The smile lasted all the way to the other side of the door. He asked himself who was really the fool.

He headed for the bar.

In all her life, Claudine had had no experience with any but the distant, abstract passion of her imagination. Perhaps you could count the mass adoration she had felt, briefly, on the runway; perhaps not. But her knowledge of love - in the actual, personal sense, and at any stratum - was vague to the extreme.

She watched him from her window as he walked down the street. When she could no longer see him, she turned to her bookshelf and took down the collected works of Simone de Beauvoir. She had never actually read these books, imagining that merely possessing them would somehow impart their contents to her. Now she opened one of the volumes: "Real love has a beak and claws," Madame had written.

Claudine closed the book, and got into her tiny bed. Sleep would not come, so she went out to her balcony and climbed onto a potted rosebush and stayed there until morning.

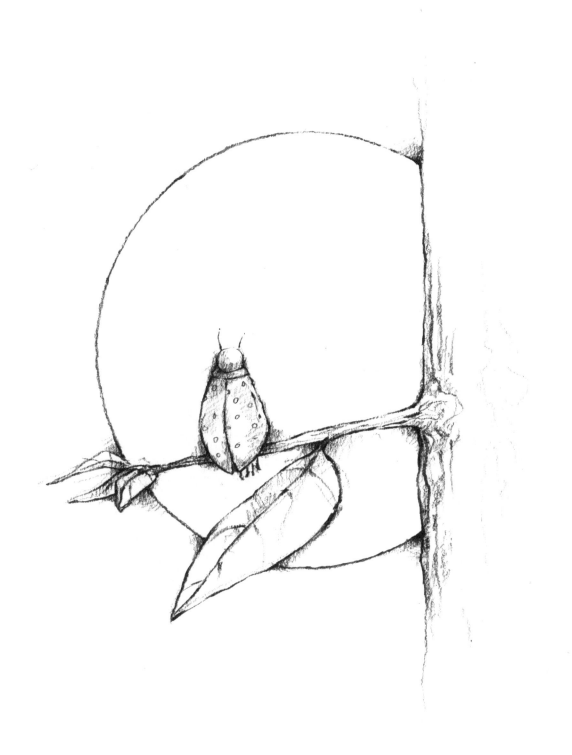

The next day, Pierre was at the offices of one Charles Chopin, producer, director, actor, composer, pioneer of cinema, and genius. Charles greeted him warmly as his secretary closed the door behind them.

Chopin was not as he appeared to be. He looked awkward, but was graceful; he looked silly, but was sharp; he looked as if he were being buffeted by the world, a mere pinball, but he was entirely in control. He was so comfortable with who he was he gave no matter to what he seemed; in fact, he enjoyed the disparity.

As they spoke, Charles balanced on his walking stick with one hand while bouncing a tennis ball back and forth with this feet and spinning a lariat with his free hand. Almost out of boredom, he lassoed his parrot who responded with the kind of graphic and foul (good grief! not everything is a pun) vitriol one would expect from one who before being adopted by Chopin had sat on a pirate's shoulder for a decade. The parrot's name was Lug. He had three livid scars on his beak. His previous owner called him his "scurvy rogue" and Lug would still be perched on this pirate's shoulder if that shoulder were not a hundred fathoms under water. Pierre detested Lug, finding him repugnant. Lug felt the same way toward Pierre; he considered him a fop.

It was easy to imagine that one of these days – oh, one of these days! Bang! Zoom! – these avian antagonists would have at.

Two days later, Pierre and Claudine stepped into that

same office. A frame or two, indeed! Chopin immediately saw in Claudine that lost look, that forlorn, confused, dazed, baffled look, that out-of place, gorgeous uncertainty audiences would embrace. He was working on a movie, now a classic, but then a mess with only a working title, "Brief Candle." The part was already in the script...

In short, Charles Chopin fell in love with her like an artist who sees in a sketch the potential for something magnificent; that was the good news. The bad news: unfortunately, Lug also fell in love with her—like the drunken, piratical parrot he was.

Claudine could feel the tension in the air. She could see the drool on Lug's beak; she could see the salacious look in his eye; she could see lots of ruffled feathers on both of the birds in the room (at least, the hint of such feathers on Pierre); she saw the leaning-in, the feral air.

Was this what acting was all about? Surely not! Surely, it was the noblest of arts - to let the camera love you, to glow upon the screen! (while, of course, casting a polite yet insistent eye on the wardrobe mistress and crew.) The only eyes she wanted on her were the camera's!

But was that so? "The little fool!" (This was Pierre's thought.) "The little fool! (This was Lug's thought.) "You little fool!" And this was Claudine's thought, about herself, for the look on Pierre's face made her waver. Where was her resolve? Her focus? Her wish to be worshipped only from afar? What did she want? She became angry—they all saw it—but they misunderstood: they thought she was angry with them. But it was she, herself, by whom she was upset, disappointed, baffled. She looked at Pierre, for help? Or perhaps longingly, but Pierre was too agitated and angry to read it as such.

Pierre had to smile and seethe for an endless ten minutes, at which time Chopin suggested a screen test. When? Why, right now! Immediately! *Tout de suite*! He practically carried her to the elevator. He said loudly, "Your audience awaits you! The world awaits you!" Claudine fluttered her eyes and echoed Chopin's words with unconvincing energy. Her future was before her. Was her heart standing behind her?

· Five ·

These pleasures we lightly call physical...
- Colette

The dressing room was a tiny, hot, airless, cluttered affair. It was more closet than room, filled with gowns, bodices, trousers, bustles, dresses, skirts, stolas, tunics, breeches, furs, ruffs, blouses, shawls, capes, pants, jackets, jumpers, kimonos, saris, kaftans, belts, stockings, aprons, vests, cloaks, hats, parasols, boas, feathers, mantelets, redingotes, and togas, from ancient Greece to Medieval Italy to Romantic Germany to Belle Epoque France to Roaring Twenties America. It was history on a wardrobe rack. A timeline with hangers. Every surface had the residue of cigarette smoke, years of it, dulling the light, dimming even the sequins on the 1920's coral hand-beaded full-sleeved mesh deco flapper dress. Claudine sat on a creaky director's chair in front of a rickety excuse for a vanity, laden with tubes and tubs of make-up and scores of bent and near-bald brushes caked with close-up residue. At any moment, Carkle Ramses will stick his head in to summon her to the set. Carkle had been Charles Chopin's assistant since Mr. Bridgeport's Gas-powered Auto-carriage, Chopin's near-classic three-reeler.

When the door opened, it was a woman's voice that spoke

with a British accent. "Oh, dear, I'm sorry. I'm looking for the loo." Pierre would have said, "You've found it, *chèrie*," but Claudine merely looked at her, gave a weak smile, and gestured down the hall.

"Are you Claudine? I've heard so much about you." The woman didn't move the door, but spoke through the small opening. "I shall be working with you. I'm the naïve house servant to the Duke. One of them, I mean. We have a scene together."

Claudine had been examining a yellowed review from The Post that had been glued to the side of the mirror:

"Mlle. Rouvin is magnificent, clearly meant for the screen, bringing life to an otherwise meager production, so much so that one is more than willing to wait patiently when she is not present. Her simultaneous transmission of gentleness and power in the final scene, standing nobly beside her now-destitute husband, laying her hand on his shoulder, yielded sobs from every soul in the audience etc., etc..."

The review had been written four years earlier and placed there by Lauren Rouvin on the eve of the movie's opening; it showed for just one weekend and Rouvin would never step onto the set again. She disappeared into the dark night, then into that very large part of history that is utterly invisible, the part known as "It Never Happened." Lauren Rouvin never happened, save for a small, frail square of paper stuck to a smoky mirror.

"I'm Molly. Fresh off the boat, as they say. I couldn't believe my good luck when Mr. Chopin chose me for his picture. I...well...I shall see you very soon on the set. I'll be the silly girl nervously holding a vase of drooping flowers about to be chastened by the butler. Though I believe he's secretly keen on me. I mean her. I am told I blush very well. And near tears, I suppose. I stammer beautifully. I shall be bewildered. Give them what they want, *n'est-ce pas?* As they say." And she closed the door.

Even Molly's shadow was beautiful.

The part Claudine remembered the least was her part. The chaos and shouting, then sudden absolute quiet and stillness, then shouting and chaos again. Not only was Claudine unsure if she had done anything right, she wasn't sure she had done anything at all. Of course, Chopin patted her on the back and said, "Splendid" about ten times. She felt like a racehorse.

The part she remembered best was Pierre's gushing over that English...lassie. The Americans had a different word for it. Disgusting! Had he no pride? She would give him what for. No, she would turn her back on him the next time her tried to speak to her.

39

Cute little, sweet little Molly: sickening. Claudine allowed her mind to imagine all manner of unfortunate disasters... If they were to shoot a scene on location, and Molly happened to be standing at the edge of a cliff...

In truth, Pierre's gushing over Molly was merely pride for a job well done: he had been responsible for her transformation - or conversion - to humankind, from that of an asp. How could Claudine know this? And, witnessing her reaction, Pierre thought he just might delay telling her. *Et pourquoi pas?* Why not?

We pause here to review the seven deadly sins, runway optional. (Pause) And now we move on.

One week later, the above qualities having enough time to ferment, Pierre was standing outside of the studio smoking a Gauloises, when he felt a drop of something land on the shoulder of his jacket. A large, gooey drop that would have been black if Pierre were a spittoon, but since he wasn't, it was – mostly – white. He looked up and saw Lug perched on the gable above him, and judging from the look of concentration on Lug's face, it was a good idea to move away from the building. Was that a grimace or a smirk on that parrot's mug?

Pierre and Lug glared at each other, and if were not imperative that his jacket be treated before Lug's goop caused a stain, he would have pummeled that supersized parrot. But attire must come first or all civilization will crumble; cooler heads must prevail. (Do not assume for one second that Pierre's decision gives credence to Lug's view of him: That is not true.

Pas vrai! Pas du tout!)

The day before the grand opening was a quiet one. The film had been finished weeks ago; all was now in the hands of those whose job it was to fill seats. Claudine and Pierre, despite all, decided to play the tourist and visit Le Palais du Baron Brux Flussard and to stroll around its Versaille-like grounds.

"Are you excited? Your first red carpet."

"I think so." Claudine had been distracted for several days. "I think so."

"The anticipation..."

"All Chopin's work. The rumors, the buzz."

A bee flew between them, right on cue.

"Nonetheless."

Claudine stopped and looked at the castle of the Baron. The moat was fifty feet wide, double that of most. Under the shadow of the machicolations and other martial projections, it was a nice stroll.

Being who she was – and sometimes all parties are prone to forgetting this – she saw things that no one else did. She stepped off the stone promenade and on to the grass. The vibration was terrific. She slid off her shoes and the vibration doubled. She closed her eyes and though she could hear Pierre's voice, it was muffled and distant; the immediate sounds came from the earth and the wind and the plants and the creatures that were the infinity that surrounded her and belonged to her. And she to them, the indispensable constituents of that infinity. And, yes, you mathematicians whom we love, we understand that there is no such thing on your blackboards as an "indispensable unit of infinity." But there should be, for none – not one – of these constituents is dispensable, is expendable. There is, dear mathematicians, a greater math.

That Claudine, standing before a grand castle, could still picture herself as Baroness with the attendant servants and wardrobe does not count in these calculations.

For Claudine realized - among other things - that whether she is a ladybug or a model or an actress or a blade of grass, she is part of this beautiful irreducible totality and her value does not change: she matters to the universe (and now perhaps to one particular member of that universe) in exactly the right proportion.

How had Claudine forgotten this? Or had she never learned?

Pierre stood by her. It took a minute for the significance of this moment to filter through his suit, but then he got it. You should have seen the smile on that wise rooster's face.

He did not interfere.

Their shadows were longer when she opened her eyes, the day cooler.

"I'm ready now," she said.

"For what?" he asked.

Her only response was to take his hand. And to smile.

Fin

Claudine's balcony

A Few Words About Our Collaboration

Imagine a line segment, point A to point B. We ask, "How many points are on this segment that is, by definition, finite?" The answer is: infinite. A numberless number of points constitute this finite, finger-long line segment.

This is what I like to call, Perfection. The immenseness, the enormity of this little thing. And here we have just defined Claudine.

Marian Grudko created this magical line segment and suggested that we connect a few of these innumerable points – some would call them, Possibilities – and see what happens. All of the points we chose for this venture were on board with the idea; none joined begrudgingly: Claudine, Pierre, the denizens of the forest and of the city, the wind, the sky, the moon, the trains and wagons, the puddles on the cobblestone streets - all gladly took their scripts in hand, and we were on our way. Thank you, Line Segment: you provided - almost - everything we needed. We just had to connect the dots. Er...points. Or is it Pierre and Claudine that have the connecting to do?

Sometimes, writers give themselves too much credit.

- t.a. young

Recently, T.A. Young wrote to me, "We should just publish our email exchanges." I have to laugh now, because several of our emails have been published - in *Claudine*. Not as emails, of course, but as important parts of the narrative. When we couldn't meet, we sent questions to each other: "Can you clarify that passage?" "What is our direction?" "I need a description." The answers became part of the book - often verbatim. Visit our Facebook page, *A Key to Claudine*. Unless we can make it to a Paris cafe, it will continue to be created via email - our own Café Littéraire.

- marian grudko